Franny
the Jelly Bean
Fairy

To Aleka, with love

Special thanks to Rachel Elliot

First published in the United Kingdom in 2017 as *Lisa the Jelly Bean Fairy* by Orchard U.K., Carmelite House, 50 Victoria Embankment, London EC4Y 0DZ.

The publisher does not have any control over and does not assume any responsibility for author or third-party websites or their content.

This book is a work of fiction. Names, characters, places, and incidents are either the product of the author's imagination or are used fictitiously, and any resemblance to actual persons, living or dead, business establishments, events, or locales is entirely coincidental.

ISBN 978-1-338-20723-1

10 9 8 7 6 5 4 3 2 1   18 19 20 21 22

Printed in the U.S.A.   40
First printing 2018

Franny
the Jelly Bean Fairy

by Daisy Meadows

SCHOLASTIC INC.

Candy Factory

The Fairyland Palace

Candy Factory Orchard

Candy Land

Wetherbur

Park

The Tree House Club

Jack Frost's Ice Castle

Animal Shelter

Community Center

Children's Hospital

Give me candy! Give me sweets!
Give me sticky, chewy treats!
Lollipops and fudge so yummy—
Bring them here to fill my tummy.

Monica, I'll steal from you.
Gabby, Franny, Shelley, too.
I will build a candy shop,
So I can eat until I pop!

Contents

Surprises

"This is a bumpy ride!" said Kirsty Tate with a laugh.

She and her best friend, Rachel Walker, giggled as they bounced up and down. Kirsty's aunt Helen patted the dashboard.

"I love this good old Candy Land van," she said. "Even if it is a little noisy and bumpy sometimes."

Candy Land was the candy factory just outside Wetherbury Village, and Aunt Helen was lucky enough to work there.

"Candy Land is my second favorite thing about Wetherbury," said Rachel.

"What's your favorite?" asked Kirsty.

"Staying with you, of course," said Rachel with a grin. "It's always magical."

Rachel had come to visit Kirsty over the school break. Ever since they had become best friends, they had also been good friends with the fairies. Magic always seemed to follow them around when they were together. Sometimes they thought that it was as if their friendship cast a very special spell.

This time, Monica the Marshmallow Fairy had whisked them away to the Fairyland Candy Factory, where candy grew on trees. They had met the other Sweet Fairies, who used their magical objects to make sure that all candy was sweet and delicious. The fairies were getting ready for the annual Harvest Feast, and asked Rachel and Kirsty if they would like to come. But then Jack Frost had appeared with his goblins. He had stolen the Sweet Fairies' magical objects so that he could keep all candy for himself.

Kirsty and Rachel had helped two of the Sweet Fairies get their magical objects back, but there were still two more to find. However, today they had something else on their minds. They were on their way to see a boy named Tal, who volunteered as a dog walker at the Wetherbury Animal Shelter.

"I can't wait to see Tal's face when he finds out that he's a winner," said Kirsty.

Candy Land had been giving its Helping Hands awards to young people who did helpful things in the community.

The girls had been helping Aunt Helen surprise the winners with special bags of Candy Land treats.

"What's inside Tal's Candy Land bag?" Rachel asked.

"Jelly beans," said Aunt Helen, smiling.

"Yum, I love jelly beans," said Kirsty.

"I brought along a small pack of them for you to share," said Aunt Helen. "You'll find them in the back of my seat."

Rachel put her hand into the pocket on the back of Aunt Helen's seat, and found the jelly bean pack. She opened it and chose a purple one.

"Grape is my favorite jelly bean flavor," she said, holding out the bag to Kirsty.

"Mine's strawberry," said Kirsty, choosing a pink one. "Thank you so much, Aunt Helen!"

Just then, Aunt Helen turned down a narrow, rutted lane. Kirsty squealed as the van went over a big bump in the road, shaking and rattling. It was even noisier than before. Smiling, the girls popped the candy into their mouths. But when they

tasted them, they got a terrible shock.

"Ugh," said Rachel.

"Yuck," said Kirsty.

Rachel pulled a tissue out of her pocket,
and both girls put the jelly beans into it.

"That wasn't strawberry flavored," said
Kirsty. "It tasted like sour milk."

"Mine was like rotten eggs," said

Rachel. "Oh no, what if Tal's jelly beans taste bad, too?"

"They're bound to," said Kirsty. "This is all Jack Frost's fault!"

They exchanged a worried look and then glanced at Aunt Helen. Because of the noisy van, she hadn't heard anything. And that was lucky, because the girls had promised never to tell anyone about Fairyland or the fairies.

Rachel and Kirsty knew exactly what was wrong with the jelly beans. The Sweet Fairies were still missing two of their magical treats. Without them, the Harvest Feast would be ruined, and so would Tal's bag of jelly beans.

The girls wanted to help, but they couldn't do it on their own.

Suddenly, Kirsty noticed something

unusual. The Helping Hands bag was
glowing. The pink and white stripes
shone as if each jelly bean inside the bag
was a tiny light.

"That's magic," Kirsty whispered in
excitement.

Rachel's heart was fluttering. No
matter how many times she shared
magical adventures with her best friend,
every time was always just as thrilling

as their very first meeting with the fairies on Rainspell Island.

Smiling, she opened the bag, and out flew Franny the Jelly Bean Fairy.

Another magical adventure was about to begin!

Three Thieves

Franny flashed a dazzling smile at the girls. Then she fluttered behind Aunt Helen's seat so that she couldn't be seen from the front of the car.

"It's good to see you both," she said. "I heard you talking about how awful your jelly beans tasted. I'm so sorry! It's because Jack Frost and the goblins have

my magical jelly bean. I want to get it
back, but I don't know where to start
looking. Will you help me?"

"Of course we will," said Rachel in a
low, determined voice.

She glanced at Aunt Helen. Luckily the noise of the van was still so loud that she hadn't noticed a thing.

"We're almost at the animal shelter," said Kirsty. "You'll have to be as quick as possible, Franny."

Hastily, she opened her backpack and let Franny flutter inside. Aunt Helen parked the van, and the girls climbed out.

The animal shelter was a long, low building. Around it, green hills rolled away in all directions. Aunt Helen led the girls toward the front door. Inside, the first thing the girls noticed was a giant jar

of jelly beans on the reception counter.
While Aunt Helen went to speak to the
receptionist, Rachel and Kirsty went to
look at the jar. There was a sign propped
up beside it.

Raise money for the animal shelter and win a
month's supply of pet food!
Guess how many jelly beans are in the jar.
One dollar per guess!

"We're here to give Tal a Candy Land's
Helping Hands award," Aunt Helen told
the receptionist.

The receptionist was wearing a name
tag that said "JB," and he gave Aunt

Helen a wide grin.

"That's great news," he said. "Tal's a real star around here. All the animals love him—he's even organized this competition to raise money."

"Candy Land was really impressed when we heard about Tal's work for the shelter," said Aunt Helen. "We've got a very big bag of candy for him."

"He's taken two of the dogs out for a walk right now," said JB. "He'll be back soon. You can wait for him here in the lobby, if you'd like."

Just then, there was a volley of barks from the back of the shelter, and JB grinned again.

"I'd better go and see what's going on," he said. "Excuse me."

As JB went out to see the dogs, Aunt Helen smiled at the girls.

"I'll just run out to the van to get Tal's bag of jelly beans," she said.

The girls looked at each other in alarm as Aunt Helen walked out.

"We can't give Tal that bag," said Kirsty with a groan. "The jelly beans are bound to taste awful."

"How can we stop Aunt Helen from handing it over?" asked Rachel.

"We have something else to worry about first," said Kirsty, pointing at the door. "Look."

Three pairs of green feet were stomping into the animal shelter. The girls looked up from the feet and saw three pairs of knobby green knees and finally the faces of three scowling goblins.

"Oh no," said Rachel. "What are goblins doing here?"

The goblins didn't notice the girls. The

goblin with the biggest feet picked up the giant jar of jelly beans from the counter and took off the lid. Then he poured every single jelly bean out of the jar into a large sack.

"That's stealing," Kirsty said, horrified.

Rachel dashed toward the goblins.

"Stop!" she cried. "Give me that bag!"

She tried to grab the sack, but the goblins snatched it out of her way.

"These jelly beans are for Jack Frost," shouted the tallest goblin. "Back to the Ice Castle!"

There was a flash of blue magic, and then the goblins and the jelly beans disappeared.

Jelly Bean Castle

Franny zoomed out of Kirsty's backpack, waving her wand. There was a burst of glittering fairy dust, and then the girls felt as if the air around them was shimmering. A wave of multicolored sparkles wrapped around them, followed by another . . . and another. The sparkles lifted Rachel and Kirsty into the air, rolling around them until they were spinning in a sea of color.

"I feel dizzy!" said Kirsty, giggling.

"I don't think I know which way is up anymore," said Rachel.

They felt their shoulders tingling, and

then beautiful fairy wings appeared.

"We're shrinking to fairy size," said Kirsty in delight.

"We have to follow the goblins," said Franny. "This is the quickest way."

The waves of sparkles rolled higher, surrounding them with color. Then there was a whooshing sound, and they felt as if they were being sucked toward the waves. Seconds later, they had left the animal shelter far behind. They twisted and turned through a whirl of colors, until at last they dropped down onto a soft gray cloud, and everything stopped spinning.

"Where are we?" asked Rachel, pushing the fluffy cloud out of her way so that she could sit up.

Kirsty fluttered her wings and looked around. Everything looked dull and fuzzy.

"Are we in Fairyland?" she asked, feeling doubtful.

"Yes," said Franny. "It's OK—we're above the Ice Castle. I brought us to a snow cloud in case Jack Frost was watching."

The three fairies fluttered to the edge of the cloud. Peeking over, they saw Jack Frost's castle below. The towers were white with a layer of frost, and the gardens stretched out toward the forest.

"Oh my goodness, look at the moat," said Rachel. "It's like a ball pit!"

Jack Frost's moat was always frozen over, but today there wasn't a glimmer of ice to be seen. Instead, the moat was completely covered with colorful jelly beans, which were piled high and hid every speck of ice.

"Look up there, behind the castle," Kirsty exclaimed.

A big hill of jelly beans was looming over the moat. Jack Frost was standing on top of it, looking down at several goblins who were lying at the bottom,

giggling. Other goblins were
sliding down the hill on
trays, sending jelly beans
flying into the air as they
landed in the moat.
"There must
be thousands of
jelly beans here,"
said Rachel in
astonishment.
"Yes, and I know
exactly how Jack
Frost has done
it," said Franny.
"Look what's
in his hand."
Rachel and
Kirsty saw a
tiny piece

of candy glowing in
the Ice Lord's hand.
They guessed right
away that it was
Franny's magical
jelly bean.

"We have to
get that magical
treat back," said
Kirsty. "But how?"

"Let's go down there and watch Jack
Frost and the goblins," said Rachel.
"Hopefully we'll see a chance to get it
back. Come on."

She, Kirsty, and Franny swooped down
to the garden, fluttering out of sight
behind the Jack Frost–shaped hedges.
They perched on the tiny branches. From
where they were standing, they could

hear Jack Frost yelling at the goblins.

"Why are you being so slow, you fools?" he shouted. "Stop jelly-bean surfing and sort every single jelly bean into separate flavors—now!"

The Ice Lord slid down the hill and started striding around the moat with his hands clasped behind his back. He glared at the goblins as they got down on their hands and knees.

"Work faster," he growled, throwing a strawberry-flavored jelly bean into the air and catching it in his mouth.

As he turned away, a goblin with a tuft of fluffy hair threw a strawberry jelly bean into his mouth, too. Jack Frost walked on, and every time he threw a jelly bean into his mouth, the goblins did the same. Then one of them missed, and

the jelly bean hit him in the eye.

"YOUCH!" he squawked.

Jack Frost whirled around and glared
at the goblin. He saw the other goblins
gobbling up the jelly beans, and his eyes
bulged angrily. His shoulders shook. His
ears twitched.

"They're mine, not yours!" he shrieked,
pointing a bony finger at the goblins.

"B-b-but they're so yummy," wailed a tall goblin.

Jack Frost snatched a yellow jelly bean out of the goblin's hand and ate it.

"Leave the jelly beans alone!" he shouted. "Every single one is for me, and only me, to eat!"

A Sweet Storm

Jack Frost turned and scrambled back up the jelly bean hill. The goblins kept on sorting the jelly beans, grumbling in louder and louder voices.

"Who wants these disgusting fruity flavors, anyway?"

"I'd rather have frosty fungus–flavored beans. Yummy!"

"Or morning moss jelly beans. Mmm, mmm!"

Rachel and Kirsty stared at the mounds of pink strawberry-flavored and purple grape-flavored jelly beans. They looked delicious.

"Look," said Kirsty, noticing something behind the pink jelly beans. "Isn't that the bag of jelly beans that the goblins stole from the animal shelter?"

Suddenly, an
idea popped
into her head.
She remembered
how dizzy she
had felt when
Franny's magic
took them from
the animal shelter.

"Maybe we can make Jack Frost
so dizzy that we will be able to take
the magical jelly bean back," she said.
"Franny, could you make jelly beans
swirl around him? All the colors might be
enough to make him feel woozy."

Franny looked at the sack of stolen jelly
beans, too, and nodded thoughtfully.

"We can use those jelly beans," she
said. "We just have to get them above

Jack Frost's head."

The three fairies fluttered down behind the pink jelly beans and hovered around the sack. They each held on to the edge of the sack, and then Franny looked at Rachel and Kirsty.

"Ready?" she said. "One ... two ...
three ... fly!"

Together, they rose up into the air,
carrying the sack with them. The
goblins saw them and squawked
in alarm, but the sack was already

out of their reach.

"We have to get to the top of the jelly bean hill," said Franny.

The sack was heavy, and it took all

their strength to flutter up to where Jack Frost was standing. The magical treat was held clutched in his hand, and it seemed to be glowing more brightly than ever. Jack Frost glared at them and narrowed his eyes.

"He's seen us," said Rachel.

"That's OK," said Franny in a brave voice.

"He doesn't know about our plan."

Jack Frost watched them coming with his arms folded across his chest, and sneered as they hovered above his head.

"You can't stop me," he said, cackling. "I'm going to eat all the jelly beans here *and* in the human world. I've got the magical jelly bean, and there's nothing you can do about it. Go ahead and drop your jelly beans on my head. I'll just eat them."

"We'll see about that," said Franny. "On the count of three—one . . . two . . . three . . . pour!"

They tilted the sack of jelly beans over Jack Frost's head, and Franny waved her wand as the jelly beans poured down. They started to swirl around Jack Frost like a mini tornado, faster and faster, until

he was almost hidden in the rainbow of
jelly bean colors.

"Stop it!" Jack Frost yelled in
frustration, waving his arms around like
windmills. "I don't like this."

"Faster!" said Franny, and the candy
tornado sped up.

Jack Frost clutched his head with his

hands, and his legs began to tremble.

"I'm so dizzy!" he wailed.

"That's what we've been waiting for," said Kirsty. "Hopefully he'll be so dizzy that we'll be able to take the magical jelly bean from him."

"I'll do it," said Rachel. "Here goes!"

She took a deep breath and zoomed into the jelly bean tornado. Kirsty and Franny watched from the outside. Rachel's hand had almost touched the magical jelly bean when Jack Frost wobbled, and ... *BONK!* He fell down onto his bottom.

"WHOA!" he

wailed as he rolled down the jelly bean hill.

His arms and legs flailed, and he turned over and over, upside down and back to front. Rachel flew over him, whizzing left and right, trying to reach the jelly bean that was clutched in his hand.

"Go away!" he yelled, blowing an enormous raspberry at her as he tumbled.

"You can do it, Rachel!" cried Kirsty, crossing her fingers.

Foul Flavors

Jack Frost tumbled over a patch of green jelly beans, and his fingers unclenched. The magical jelly bean flew out of his hand and went spinning into the air.

"Catch it, you fools!" Jack Frost roared at his goblins.

Jabbering and squealing, the goblins scrambled over the jelly beans, reaching

their arms up into the air. Franny
zoomed after the magical treat, too,
swerving to avoid the jumping goblins as
they tried to stop her.

"Look!" said Kirsty from behind the
goblins, in her loudest voice. "A frosty
fungus jelly bean!"

Right away, the
goblins spun around
and dashed toward
Kirsty, licking their
lips and drooling.
As they stampeded
toward Kirsty
and away from
the magical jelly
bean, Franny caught
it in her outstretched
hands. It immediately
shrank to fairy size.

"Yes!" cried Rachel,
cheering.

Kirsty fluttered
into the air, and the
goblins howled. Jack
Frost roared and

stamped his feet in fury.

"I want the magical jelly bean!" he bellowed. "Give it back. I want all the jelly beans in the world!"

"You couldn't possibly eat all the jelly beans in the world," said Kirsty.

"Oh, yes I could," said Jack Frost in a sulky voice. "And I'll prove it."

He started to shove jelly beans into

his mouth. The goblins watched, licking
their lips, as Jack Frost began to munch
his way through the jelly bean hill. At
first he ate quickly, chewing as fast as
he could ram the candy into his mouth.
But then Kirsty noticed
something strange.

"All of a sudden,
Jack Frost doesn't
look quite so blue,"
she said.

"He's turning . . .
green!" said Rachel,
gasping.

Jack Frost chewed
slower and slower,
until his mouth
hung open and jelly

beans spilled out of it. He clutched his tummy.

"I don't feel very well," he said.

"I'm not surprised," said Rachel, fluttering toward him. "Nobody is supposed to eat that many jelly beans on their own. Why don't you share them with the goblins?"

"Good idea," said one of the goblins.

"What a wise fairy," said another.

Jack Frost scowled, and then let out a loud burp, and groaned.

"All right, all right," he said finally, in a grumpy voice.

The goblins whooped and cheered, and then they raised their arms above their heads and dove headfirst into the jelly bean hill. Franny waved her wand again, and more jelly beans rained down on the group of goblins.

"Frosty fungus and morning moss flavors," said Franny with a smile.

"I think these jelly beans are going to keep them happy for a long time," said Rachel, smiling.

"I hope so," said Franny. "Now, I'm going to take you both back to the animal shelter. I think you have a fun job waiting for you there!"

She raised her wand above her head,
and a shower of silvery fairy dust burst
from it like a fountain. The silver floated
down and landed on the fairies, making
their hair and wings glitter. It even dusted
their eyelashes, so that everything they
looked at seemed to be glimmering. Then
the silvery sparkles faded, and they were

once again standing next to the reception desk of the animal shelter. They were human again, and Franny was fluttering beside them. Not a single second had passed in the human world since they had left.

The girls looked around and saw that the giant jar was still empty.

"Quick, Franny, the jelly bean jar!" Kirsty exclaimed.

With a flick of her wand, Franny filled
the giant jar to the brim.

"Thank you, my friends," she said,
smiling at them. "I'm so happy to have
my magical jelly bean back. I can't
wait to show the other Sweet Fairies.
I couldn't have done it without you."

"We love being able to help," said
Rachel.

"I'll see you at the Harvest Feast,"
said the little fairy. "It's
my favorite time of
year! I can't wait
to play party
games with you,
and let you taste
all the amazing
treats that we have
grown."

She waved, and then disappeared back to Fairyland in a flurry of magical sparkles.

Rachel and Kirsty hugged each other and smiled happily.

A Reward for Kindness

As Franny's last sparkles disappeared, the door of the animal shelter opened, and Aunt Helen came back in. She was carrying the special Candy Land's Helping Hands bag of jelly beans, and had a big smile on her face.

"Here's Tal's prize," she said, her eyes shining with excitement. "You should take it, girls. I'd like you to be the ones to present it to Tal."

Rachel and Kirsty held the bag between them, and looked down at the pile of gleaming, colorful jelly beans. They shared a secret smile, thinking about how Franny had been inside that bag just a short time ago.

"They look delicious," said Kirsty.

"And now we know that they're going to taste delicious, too," said Rachel, smiling with relief.

Just then, they heard happy barking, and two golden retrievers bounded in. They ran up to the girls, wagging their tails. Rachel laughed and patted them.

"You two remind me of my dog, Buttons," she said.

"They're great, aren't they?" said the boy who had followed them in.

The two dogs turned and weaved around the boy's legs, leaning against him and panting happily.

"They're saying thank you because I just took them

for a walk," he said, smiling and gently rubbing their ears.

Rachel and Kirsty exchanged a knowing smile. They knew that this had to be Tal.

"What are their names?" Kirsty asked.

"Candy and Sweetie," the boy replied. "And I'm Tal."

Before the girls could introduce themselves, the door at the back of the shelter opened, and JB came in with another man and a woman.

"Ah, I see you've found Tal," he said. "This is Mark and Niki, and they work here at the shelter, too. When I told them why you were here, they wanted to come along, too."

Tal looked around with a confused expression. He couldn't understand why

everyone was smiling at him. Then
Rachel and Kirsty stepped forward.

"Tal, everyone here would like to
reward you for your kindness and
helpfulness," said Kirsty.

"Your friends told the people at Candy

Land about all the volunteer work you do here," said Rachel. "You're super kind to all the animals, and you walk them every day, no matter what the weather's like or how tired you are."

"My aunt Helen asked us to give you this," said Kirsty. "She works at Candy Land, and you have won their Helping Hands award. Congratulations, Tal!"

Together, Rachel and Kirsty handed the big bag of candy to Tal. His mouth fell open, and his cheeks went pink. JB, Niki, Mark, and Aunt Helen clapped.

"Thank you," Tal said. "I can't believe it! Jelly beans are my absolute favorite candy in the world."

"You deserve it," said Rachel, giving Tal a big smile.

Tal grinned, and then put the jelly beans on the desk.

"Before I get my treat, my friends deserve theirs," he said.

He reached down behind the desk and pulled out a jar of healthy doggie treats. Soon, Candy and Sweetie were crunching bone-shaped biscuits and wagging their tails even harder than before. Then Tal offered his jelly beans around to everyone before taking one himself.

"I got a pink one," said Kirsty, popping it into her mouth. "Mmm, it's strawberry. Delicious!"

"Mine's grape," said Rachel, who had chosen a purple one. "These are yummy."

"Much better than morning moss or frosty fungus," Kirsty added in a whisper.

Rachel looked around. Everyone else was chatting with Tal. She could talk to Kirsty without being overheard.

"I keep thinking about the jelly beans that are growing in the orchard at the

Fairyland Candy Factory," she said. "Do you remember how bright and shiny and tasty they looked?"

Kirsty nodded.

"I bet that the fairies are busy picking the candy for their Harvest Feast tomorrow," she said. "Oh, Rachel, I hope

that we can help get the last magical treat back from Jack Frost before then."

"We have to," said Rachel, feeling determined. "We can't let Jack Frost spoil the fairies' special day. Don't worry. The Harvest Feast is going to be amazing, and I can't wait to be part of it!"

RAINBOW magic
THE SWEET FAIRIES

Rachel and Kirsty have found Monica,
Gabby, and Franny's missing magical items.
Now it's time for them to help

Shelley
the Sugar Fairy!

Join their next adventure in
this special sneak peek . . .

An Extra Present

Rachel Walker was sitting at the bottom of the stairs in the house of her best friend, Kirsty Tate, fastening her party shoes.

"It's nice of your friend from school to invite me to her birthday party, too," said Rachel.

"Anna knows how excited I am to have you staying with me for a whole week," Kirsty said, smiling. "She's looking forward to meeting you."

Rachel jumped to her feet and smoothed down her party dress.

"I'm ready," she said. "Let's go."

Kirsty put their presents for Anna into a bag and then opened the front door. To her surprise, she saw her aunt Helen standing there.

"Oh!" said Aunt Helen. "How lucky —I was just about to knock. My goodness, you two look sharp!"

"We're on our way

to my friend Anna Goldman's birthday party," Kirsty explained.

"I know," said Aunt Helen. "Actually, I'm here to give you a ride to the party. You see, Anna has won a Candy Land

Helping Hands award, and I was hoping that you would present it to her."

Kirsty clapped her hands together in delight.

"This will be a really perfect birthday surprise for Anna," she said. "She has raised lots of money for the Wetherbury Children's Hospital."

Aunt Helen worked at Candy Land, a candy factory in town. She was in charge of organizing the Helping Hands awards, which were special gift bags of candy for local children who did helpful things around the community. Kirsty and Rachel had been helping her present the awards all week.

Kirsty and Rachel said good-bye to Mr. and Mrs. Tate, and then jumped into Aunt Helen's Candy Land van. It didn't take long

to reach the Wetherbury community center.

"Wow, the community center looks amazing," said Kirsty.

Rachel looked up. Colorful balloons were tied to the building's railings, and there were more around the doorway. A huge banner above the door said HAPPY

BIRTHDAY, ANNA!

"I'm good friends with Anna's mom," said Aunt Helen. "We got up early this morning and came here to decorate. I'm still shaking glitter out of my hair!"

The girls laughed as they got out of the van. Aunt Helen stayed in her seat.

"Aren't you coming in?" Kirsty asked.

"I'll be back soon," said Aunt Helen. "First, I'm going to Candy Land to pick up Anna's cake. Her mom told me that her favorite dessert is popping candy, so her Helping  Hands award is a special popping candy birthday cake. I'll bring it here for the end of the party, and you can both help me surprise Anna."

As soon as the girls heard the words

"popping candy," they exchanged a
worried glance. Luckily, Aunt Helen didn't
notice. The girls waved good-bye as she
drove off. Then they walked up the path
to the community center, carrying the
bag holding their presents between them.

"I'd forgotten how much Anna likes
popping candy," said Kirsty in a low
voice. "I hope her cake isn't ruined by
Jack Frost and his terrible goblins!"

Which Magical Fairies Have You Met?

❑ The Rainbow Fairies
❑ The Weather Fairies
❑ The Jewel Fairies
❑ The Pet Fairies
❑ The Sports Fairies
❑ The Ocean Fairies
❑ The Princess Fairies
❑ The Superstar Fairies
❑ The Fashion Fairies
❑ The Sugar & Spice Fairies
❑ The Earth Fairies
❑ The Magical Crafts Fairies
❑ The Baby Animal Rescue Fairies
❑ The Fairy Tale Fairies
❑ The School Day Fairies
❑ The Storybook Fairies
❑ The Friendship Fairies

SCHOLASTIC

HiT entertainment

Find all of your favorite fairy friends at
scholastic.com/rainbowmagic

RMFAIRY17

RAINBOW magic™ SPECIAL EDITION

Which Magical Fairies Have You Met?

- ❏ Joy the Summer Vacation Fairy
- ❏ Holly the Christmas Fairy
- ❏ Kylie the Carnival Fairy
- ❏ Stella the Star Fairy
- ❏ Shannon the Ocean Fairy
- ❏ Trixie the Halloween Fairy
- ❏ Gabriella the Snow Kingdom Fairy
- ❏ Juliet the Valentine Fairy
- ❏ Mia the Bridesmaid Fairy
- ❏ Flora the Dress-Up Fairy
- ❏ Paige the Christmas Play Fairy
- ❏ Emma the Easter Fairy
- ❏ Cara the Camp Fairy
- ❏ Destiny the Rock Star Fairy
- ❏ Belle the Birthday Fairy
- ❏ Olympia the Games Fairy
- ❏ Selena the Sleepover Fairy

- ❏ Cheryl the Christmas Tree Fairy
- ❏ Florence the Friendship Fairy
- ❏ Lindsay the Luck Fairy
- ❏ Brianna the Tooth Fairy
- ❏ Autumn the Falling Leaves Fairy
- ❏ Keira the Movie Star Fairy
- ❏ Addison the April Fool's Day Fairy
- ❏ Bailey the Babysitter Fairy
- ❏ Natalie the Christmas Stocking Fairy
- ❏ Lila and Myla the Twins Fairies
- ❏ Chelsea the Congratulations Fairy
- ❏ Carly the School Fairy
- ❏ Angelica the Angel Fairy
- ❏ Blossom the Flower Girl Fairy
- ❏ Skyler the Fireworks Fairy
- ❏ Giselle the Christmas Ballet Fairy
- ❏ Alicia the Snow Queen Fairy

■ SCHOLASTIC
Find all of your favorite fairy friends at
scholastic.com/rainbowmagic

3 stories in each one!

HIT entertainment

RMSPECIAL20